Ireland
BEYOND THE PALE

a photo-essay by

Pádraig Ó Flannabhra

Introduction by John Montague

The Dolmen Press

Set in Palatino type by Redsetter Limited
and produced by Keats European Production Limited
for the publishers,
The Dolmen Press
Mountrath, Portlaoise, Ireland

Designed by Liam Miller
First published 1986
ISBN 0 85105 448 X

A Menaced Stillness

OUR JOURNEY BEGINS QUIETLY, with a boat waiting under trees. Where shall we go, but through the four green fields? But this sleepy stillness is deceptive, these late days. Will a vision tremble the thorn tree? Are those four milk churns harmless? Take a sidestep into a white-washed cottage and you may find yourself inside a folk village, Cultra or Bunratty.

The only unchanging thing in our world is change. Four tinker children cajole, pout or ignore us but behind them looms a convoy of cars and caravans, not horse drawn and decorated, but shining and motorised. Four is a motif in the opening movement of this book which is one man's view of four provinces. Padraig, the photographer, is from Pocan, County Tipperary, a still point from which to observe the Ireland of the Eighties.

The Ronald Reagan Roadshow meets its expected receptions, hostile and official, surveyed by a girl with a profile of Egypt. Our guide's humour is sly, shy, puckish, all pervasive. Thatcher here may still mean a man carrying scallops, the wrinkles on his forehead contrasting with the lines of the rods, the ladder like a diagonal in the background. Perhaps he is the father of the beauty, Nefertiti? Or the inscrutable Aeneas?

These are timeless images but others tick with the specific trouble of our times. A happy captain holds a cup aloft but behind it beckons a billboard for the emigrant boats to Britain. A more desperate game is being played where the youthful, smiling faces of the dying hungerstrikers line up underneath an advertisement – Player's Please. The terrible trinity of forces identified by Daniel Corkery – religion, nationalism and land – are never far away.

But the pictures leave us to draw our own conclusions, whether the image be bleak, yet blossoming, like that Beckettian border tree in Youghal, or hilarious as a mop of Orangemen clearing the way under a sign: JET SET. Patrick Kavanagh joked about Radio Iran but as statues move and amendments fail perhaps Ireland is becoming a haven of fanaticism, a last ditch land.

Like that bull brooding over the fence you have to be all eyes, all ears to hear the moo-*sic* of what happens. Joyce's light joke about *Chamber Music* resounds as a Powder Room in a Point-to-Point field, or nuns chatting outside a hastily named Gaelic Ladies. These subtle pictures will help you to pick your way through the mind field of Ireland, old as Newgrange or Eamhain Macha, upbeat as Monsignor Horan welcoming jets to the West, while a great traditional or *sean nós* singer is laid to rest, like a hero of ancient times.

John Montague

In a Quiet Watered Land
Hogan's Quay, Lough Derg, County Tipperary.

2

Four Green Fields
Blessed Bush, Urra-Hill,
County Tipperary.

Lids Off
Milk Churns, Ballinderry,
County Tipperary.

4

Side Step
Country Style, Burgess,
County Tipperary.

5

News From America
Bunratty, County Clare.

Any Change
Itinerant Children, Carlow.

No Change
Traditional Grocery and Morris Minor, County Galway.

Greenpeace
Anti Nuclear Protest, Ballyporeen.

Intervention
Céad Míle Fáilte to Ballyporeen.

Nefertiti
Aran Clad spectator, Ballyporeen.

Stage and Screen
President and Mrs. Reagan at home in Ballyporeen.

12

Summer-time
Killorglin, County Kerry.

Thatcher
Man with Scallops, Pocán, County Tipperary.

Up for the Match
Cork v Offaly, Centenary All Ireland, Thurles.

Still in Stitches
Centenary Captains:
Noel Skehan, Jack Lynch, Eddie Keher, Thurles.

16

Ship Shape
Kerry Football Captain,
Ambrose O'Donovan, All
Ireland Centenary Final
Croke Park, Dublin.

Up In Arms
GAA Supporters,
Munster Final, Thurles.

Watchmen
From the Pier, An Spidéal, Conndae na Gaillimhe.

The Way Forward
Rásaí na gCurrachtaí, An Spidéal.

The 'Field'
Punters, Point-to-Point, Nenagh.

Tree of Knowledge
Point-to-Point Races, Nenagh.

Powder Room
Womens Convenience,
Point-to-Point, Nenagh.

Hand Over Fist
A Quincentennial Bet,
Galway Races.

24

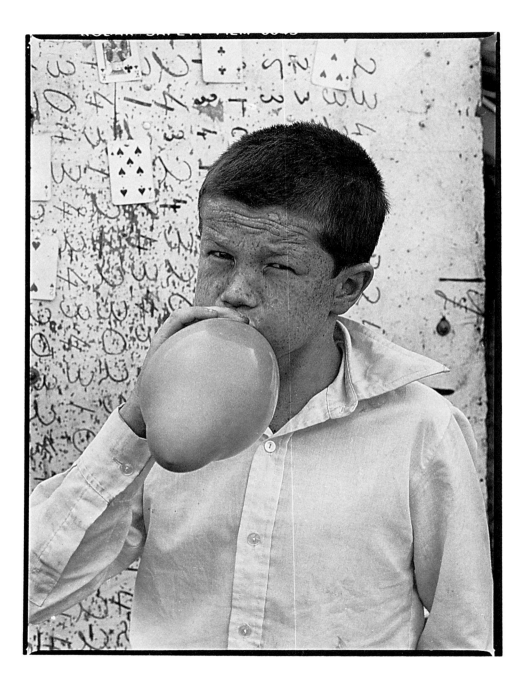

Blow-Up
Boy with Balloon,
Galway Races.

Last Race
End of the day,
Galway Races.

The Lark in the Clear Air
Street Musicians, Salthill, County Galway.

Preab 'San Aer
Bradley Mór: Dancer,
An Spidéal, Conndae na
Gaillimhe.

28

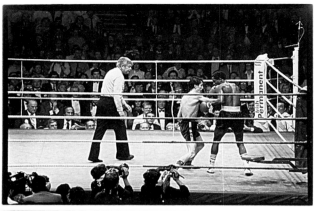

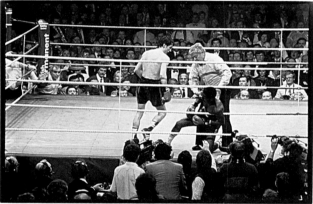

Ring of Defence
McGuigan defends his title,
R.D.S., Dublin.

Joint Authority
Barry and Sandra McGuigan, Press Conference, Dublin.

Charlie is an Angel
Feast of Corpus Christi,
Mitchel Street, Nenagh.

An Eye For An Eye
Puck Fair, Killorglin,
County Kerry.

On the Way to the Forum
Castleisland Caper, County Kerry.

Outside the Kingdom
Inauguration of Dr. Dermot Clifford (Kerry)
Coadjutor Bishop, Cashel.

Close Encounters
Self Portrait, Birr, County Offaly.

Love, Counter Love
Mr. & Mrs. Gerry Irvine's shop, Kickham Street, Nenagh.

36

Winner Alright
Fianna Fáil leader, Charles
J. Haughey T.D.

Opinion Polls
Young and Wise Observers,
County Tipperary.

38

A Bird in the Hand
Turkey Market, Kenyon
Street, Nenagh.

Mini-Market
Birr, County Offaly.

Norman Conquest
Siamsa Cois Laoi, Cork.

Sunday World
Crossing the Road, Templeglantine, County Limerick.

Me Doubts
Moving Statue,
Ballinspittle, County Cork.

Seeing is Believing
Moving Cross and People,
Ballinspittle.

Stocking Up
Holy Water on Tap, Knock, County Mayo.

Spiritual Refreshment
Souvenir Shop, Knock.

Holy Souls
Stations of the Cross,
Knock.

Without Camels
Our Lady's Island, Pilgrimage, County Wexford.

Summit Progress
Down at the Reek, Croagh Patrick, County Mayo.

Amendment
Young girl meditating,
Croagh Patrick.

Waiting
Before the hearse arrives, Connemara.

Backchat
Cómhrá idir Cáirde, Connemara.

Over
Funeral of Sean Nós Singer, Seosamh Ó h-Éanaí, Carna.

Faithful Departed
Headstones, Tír-Dhá-Ghlas, County Tipperary.

In Loving Memory
Monumental Sculpture, Nenagh.

Happy Days
Eochaill, County Cork.

Red Branch Knights
New Ireland Group, Eamhain Macha, County Armagh.

Northern Lights
Hunger Strikers' Republican Window, Nenagh.

Lap-Dog
Country Lady and Pet
Puppy.

All my Trust in Thee
Charles Haughey T.D. and
Bishop Cathal B. Daly,
New Ireland Forum,
Dublin Castle.

60

Beat It!
Lambeg Drummer,
12th July Orange Parade,
County Down.

Son of Ulster
Genteel Loyalist,
Banbridge, County Down.

62

In Ages Past

At Prayer: The Rev. Dr. Ian
Kyle Paisley, Courthouse
Steps, Hillsborough.

Out of Ink
Anglo-Irish Agreement, Hillsborough Castle, County Down.

Talking to the Wall
Heifer, West of Ireland.

Leading the Mop
Orange Parade, Banbridge, County Down.

Under Cover
Hawker, North Tipperary
Show Day, Nenagh.

Aeneas
All dressed up and
enjoying a smoke, Nenagh.

Double Glazing
The light-box, Newgrange 3000 B.C., County Meath.

Double Glazing
The light-box, Newgrange A.D. 1983, County Meath.

Out of Order
Nuns Dilemma, Thurles,
County Tipperary.

Ecumenical Gathering
Punks between the Churches, Banbridge.

Inaugural Airwave
Monsignor James Horan.

Wings
Connaught Regional Airport, Knock.

The Economy
Looking out Beyond the Pale.